Too Many Tables

Written by Abraham Schroeder

Illustrated by Micah Monkey

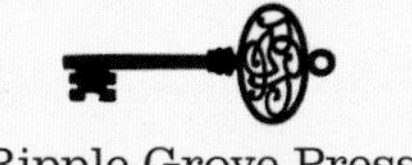

Ripple Grove Press

FRENCH BISTRO
FRENCH BISTRO
FRENCH BISTRO
BISTRO
BISTRO
OPENING TONIGHT

The restaurant was almost ready to open.

Months of careful preparation had gone into every detail to make sure it was the best restaurant ever.

The chef had chosen the best pots and pans in gleaming bright copper and steel.

The menu had been lovingly chosen and carefully refined to please everyone, from the pickiest eaters to those with the most adventurous of palates.

The designer selected the perfect lights, paint, and wallpaper, and a beautiful new floor, to give the space a fresh look, ready to wow customers from day one and for years to come.

The owners came in to check on the progress.

Everything was perfect.

"We are all ready for a grand opening!"

However, there was one big problem that nobody noticed . . .

"Where are the tables?"
FRENCH BISTRO
FRENCH BISTRO

"We need tables!"
The chef said,
"I'll ask around to see if anyone
has tables we can use."
The baker said,
"I'll ask around to
see if anyone has
tables we can use."

The designer said,
"I'll ask around to see
if anyone has tables
we can use."
And everyone
on the waitstaff said,
"We'll ask around to see
if anyone has tables
we can use."

FRENCH BISTRO
Moments later, there was a knock on the restaurant door.
"I heard that you need tables. Here is one you can use."
"Thank you! This is a huge help!"

A few minutes later,
there was another knock.
"I brought you this table
for your restaurant."
"Thank you!
We need tables
very badly!"
Not long after, there
was another knock.
"Somebody told me that
you need some tables.
I had an extra,
so please use it."
"Thank you!"

For the rest of the morning a steady stream of people came to the door delivering tables.

They brought very small tables and very large tables, old tables and new tables, simple tables and fancy tables, dining room tables and kitchen tables.

The staff rushed to put the tables in place.

Before long, the restaurant had all the tables it needed!

"Wow! Thanks to the generosity of all these wonderful people, we have just enough tables."

CAFE

Table of Contents
PERIODIC TABLE

But people with tables kept coming.

They brought short tables
and tall tables,
coffee tables
and patio tables,
folding tables and
foosball tables,
Ping-Pong tables
and pool tables.

The staff started putting tables in the kitchen.

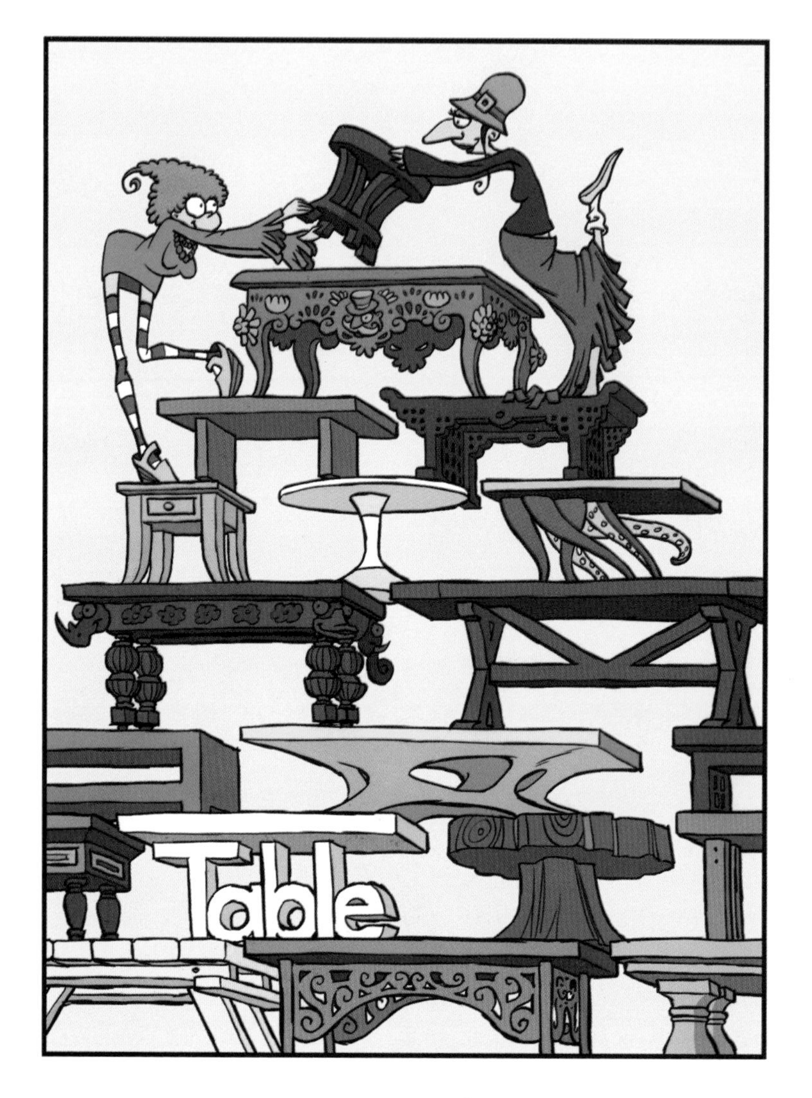

They started stacking tables on top of one another.

They started setting tables outside.

They started carrying tables to the roof.

The chef said,
"There are too many tables!"
The baker said,
"There are too many tables!"

The designer said,
"There are too many tables!"
And everyone on the waitstaff said,
"There are just
TOO MANY TABLES!"

"HOLD ON, EVERYBODY!"

the owners shouted.

"Thank you all SO much for your help in finding tables,
but, as you can see, we have far too many tables now!
We can't open a restaurant with too many tables.
There is no room for food or people!
We need to get rid of some of these tables.
Please spread the word to everyone
to start taking tables away!"

In a short time, the flow of tables coming in

was changed to a flow of tables going out.

A steady stream of people were taking tables away.

They took tables off the roof

and out of the tree.

They took tables off other tables

and out of the kitchen.

Before long, the restaurant was looking more like a restaurant. The owners said, "I think we have just enough tables! Just exactly the right number! Thank you for your help. You can stop taking tables away!" Everybody cheered! The restaurant was now REALLY ready to open!

"Wait a second . . ."

"Where are the chairs?"